Where's Spot?

Eric Hill

PUFFIN

Naughty Spot! It's dinner time. Where can he be?

Is he
behind
the door?

Is he inside the clock?

Is he
in the
piano?

Is he under the stairs?

Is he
in the wardrobe?

Is he under the bed?

Is he
in the
box?

There's Spot!

He's
under the
rug.

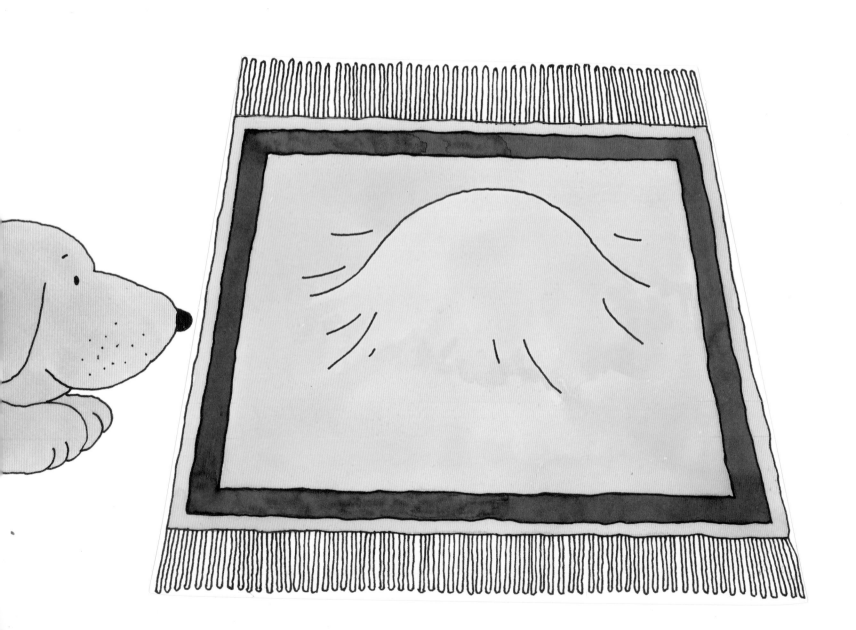

Good boy, Spot.
Eat up your dinner!

PUFFIN BOOKS

Published by the Penguin Group: London, New York,
Australia, Canada, India, Ireland, New Zealand and South Africa
Penguin Books Ltd, Registered Offices:
80 Strand, London WC2R 0RL, England

puffinbooks.com

First published by William Heinemann Ltd 1980
Published in Puffin Books 1983
This edition published 2013

005

Copyright © Eric Hill, 1980
All rights reserved

The moral right of the author/illustrator has been asserted

Printed and bound in China

ISBN: 978–0–141–34374–7